Off You Go!

written by Jay Dale

illustrated by Cherie Zamazing

Tim did not like
to clean his teeth.

"No!" he said,
with a *stomp*, *stomp*, *stomp*!

3

"Off you go
and clean your teeth!"
said Grandpa Josh.

4

Off Tim went to clean his teeth.

Tim did not like
to brush his hair.

"No!" he said,
with a *stomp, stomp, stomp!*

6

"Off you go
and brush your hair!"
said Grandpa Josh.

Off Tim went to brush his hair.

9

Tim did not like
to wash his face.

"No!" he said,
with a *stomp*, *stomp*, *stomp*!

"Off you go
and wash your face!"
said Grandpa Josh.

12

Off Tim went to wash his face.

"Look at me!"
said Tim to Grandpa Josh.
"I look good!"

Grandpa Josh looked at Tim.
"Off you go ..."

15

"...to basketball!"

16